A Christmas Carol

Charles Dickens

Condensed and Adapted by
W.T. ROBINSON

Illustrated by
JASON ALEXANDER

Cover Illustrated by
LARRY SCHWINGER

bendon

The Junior Classics have been
adapted and illustrated with care and thought
to introduce you to a world of famous authors, characters, ideas,
and great stories that have been loved for generations.

Editor — Kathryn Knight
Creative Director — Gina Rhodes Haynes
And the entire classics project team

A CHRISTMAS CAROL

Copyright © 2014 Bendon
Ashland, Ohio 44805 • 1-888-5-BENDON
bendonpub.com

Printed in the United States of America

A note to the reader—

A classic story rests in your hands. The characters are famous. The tale is timeless.

This Junior Classic edition of *A Christmas Carol* has been carefully condensed and adapted from the original version (which you really *must* read when you're ready for every detail). We kept the well-known phrases for you. We kept Charles Dickens's style. And we kept the important imagery and heart of the tale.

Literature is terrific fun! It encourages you to think. It helps you dream. It is full of heroes and villains, suspense and humor, adventure and wonder, and new ideas. It introduces you to writers who reach out across time to say: "Do you want to hear a story I wrote?"

Curl up and enjoy.

CONTENTS

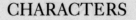

EBENEZER SCROOGE — a mean, stingy old man who declares that Christmas is a humbug

BOB CRATCHIT— Scrooge's trusty clerk

NEPHEW FRED — Scrooge's cheery nephew who comes to wish him a Merry Christmas

BUSINESSMEN — local men who come to ask Scrooge to donate to the needy for Christmas

The Spirits
    JACOB MARLEY — Scrooge's former business partner who had died seven years before on Christmas Eve
    FIRST SPIRIT — Ghost of Christmas Past
    SECOND SPIRIT — Ghost of Christmas Present
    THIRD SPIRIT — Ghost of Christmas Yet To Come

In Scrooge's Past
    FANNY — Scrooge's little sister (Fred's future mother) who adores her brother
    OLD FEZZIWIG — Scrooge's fun-loving boss
    DICK WILKINS — Fezziwig's other assistant
    BELLE — Scrooge's beloved he plans to marry

CHARACTERS

In Scrooge's Present

MRS. CRATCHIT — Bob's wife. The Cratchits have six children, including Martha, Belinda, Peter, and...

TINY TIM — the youngest Cratchit who is crippled and frail

FRED'S PARTY — Nephew Fred, his wife, her sisters, Topper, and guests celebrating Christmas

In Scrooge's Future

MERCHANTS — a group of businessmen discussing and laughing about a man who has died

OLD JOE — a buyer and seller of stolen goods

THIEVES — a cleaning woman, a laundry woman, and an undertaker's man who are selling goods stolen from a man who has died

CAROLINE — wife and mother to a family in debt to a man who, she is happy to hear, has died

BOY IN SUNDAY CLOTHES — lad who fetches a turkey for Scrooge on Christmas morn

A Christmas Carol

CHAPTER ONE

Ebenezer Scrooge

Marley was dead, to begin with. There is no doubt about that. The burial papers were signed by the minister, the clerk, and the undertaker.

Did Scrooge know Marley was dead? Of course he did. He must have known. Scrooge and Marley were business partners for I-don't-know-how-many years. Scrooge arranged his funeral, took care of his Will, and inherited his share of the company. But Scrooge was not too shaken up by the sad event. For, on the very day of the funeral, he hurried back to his office to work on a business deal. Making money was more important to Scrooge than the memory of a lost friend.

Old Marley was as dead as a doornail.

Now, I don't mean to say that I know what is so dead about a doornail. I would think that a coffin nail would be the deadest nail there is. But I am not going to argue with our ancestors who made up this saying. So, let me repeat that Marley was as dead as a doornail. That must be clearly understood, or you won't find anything strange and wonderful about the story I am going to tell.

Scrooge never bothered to take Marley's name off the sign above the office door. There it stood, years afterward: SCROOGE AND MARLEY. Sometimes people new to the business called Scrooge "Scrooge," and sometimes "Marley." He answered to both names. It didn't seem to matter to him.

Oh, what a stingy tightwad of a businessman Scrooge was! A squeezing, penny-pinching, greedy old sinner! Hard and cold as steel, and private and secret as an oyster in its shell. The cold within him showed on the outside, too. It nipped his pointed nose, shriveled his cheek, and stiffened his walk. It made his eyes red, his thin lips blue, and his voice raspy. His hair and his eyebrows were frosty white, as if his cold heart had frozen them.

Outside heat and cold had little effect on Scrooge. No summer heat could warm him; no wintry weather could chill him. No wind that blew was bitterer than he, and no snow or sleet more harsh and unforgiving. But the heaviest snow or hail or sleet had one advantage over him: Sooner or later they warmed up and changed their icy form—Scrooge never did.

Nobody ever stopped him in the street to say, with friendly looks, "My dear Scrooge, how are you? When will you come to see me?"

No beggars asked him for a small gift. No children asked him what time it was. No one ever asked directions of him.

Did Scrooge care? No. He enjoyed warning all human kindness to stay away from him.

Once upon a time—of all the good days in the year, on Christmas Eve—old Scrooge sat busy in his office. It was cold, biting, foggy weather, and he could hear the people in the street outside, puffing up and down and stamping their feet to warm them. The bells in the city clocks had only just rung THREE, but it was quite dark already. The fog was so thick that the houses on the other side of the narrow street were only faint shapes.

Scrooge kept his private office door open so that he could keep his eye on his clerk. His clerk sat in his own small, gloomy office copying letters. Scrooge had a very small fire, but the clerk's fire was so very much smaller that it looked like one coal. But the clerk couldn't add to it, for Scrooge kept the coal box in his own room. If the clerk asked for even one more piece of coal, Scrooge would threaten to fire him from his job. So the poor, shivering clerk put on his white scarf and sat a little closer to his candle, thinking that might help.

"Merry Christmas, uncle! God bless you!" cried a cheerful voice. It was the voice of Scrooge's nephew, who had come in so quickly that Scrooge had not noticed him.

"Bah!" said Scrooge. "Humbug! Nonsense! Christmas means nothing to me. It's a time of foolishness, and that's why I call it Humbug!"

"Christmas a humbug, uncle?" said Scrooge's nephew. "You don't mean that, I am sure?"

"I do," said Scrooge. "Merry Christmas? Why should *you* be merry? You're poor enough."

"Come, then," said the nephew cheerily. "Why should *you* be gloomy? You're rich enough."

Scrooge, having no other answer right on the tip of his tongue, said "Bah!" again, and followed it up with "Humbug!"

"Don't be cross, uncle," said the nephew.

"What else can I be," said Scrooge, "when I live in such a world of fools? Merry Christmas! Merry Christmas, indeed! What's Christmas time to you but a time for paying bills without money? A time for finding yourself a year older, but not an hour richer? If I could have my way, every idiot who goes around saying 'Merry Christmas' would be boiled with his own pudding, and buried with a holly branch stuck through his heart!"

"Uncle!" pleaded the nephew.

"Nephew," said the uncle firmly, "you celebrate Christmas in *your* way, and let me celebrate it in *mine*!"

"Celebrate it?" repeated Scrooge's nephew. "But you *don't* celebrate it."

"Let me leave it alone, then," said Scrooge. "And how much good has it done *you*? How much good will it *ever* do you?"

"Christmas may not put money in my pocket," answered the nephew, "but it has always been a *good* time—a loving, forgiving, pleasant time.

It is a time to remember the Holy Birth. It is a time of the year when people are kind to one another—sharing with one another. Therefore, uncle, I believe that it *has* done me good, and *will* do me good. And I say, God bless it!"

The clerk in the tiny office next door could not keep from clapping his hands, though he knew right away this was a mistake.

"Let me hear another sound from you in there," shouted Scrooge, "and you'll celebrate *your* Christmas by losing your job!"

Scrooge's nephew spoke up. "Don't be angry, uncle. Come! Have dinner with us tomorrow."

Scrooge said he would not.

"But why?" cried the nephew. "Why? I want nothing from you. Why can't we be friends?"

"I've told you what I think of Christmas," said Scrooge. "Now, please leave. Good afternoon."

"I am sorry, with all my heart, to find you so stubborn. But at least I tried. Out of respect for Christmas, I tried, and I'll keep my Christmas spirit. So, a MERRY CHRISTMAS, uncle!"

"Good afternoon," said Scrooge.

"And a HAPPY NEW YEAR!"

"Go, and leave me alone!" shouted Scrooge.

His nephew left the room, but without an angry word, in spite of his uncle's meanness. He stopped on his way out to give a Christmas greeting to the clerk (who, cold as he was, was warmer than Scrooge, for he returned the greeting cheerfully).

"There's *another* fool," muttered Scrooge, who overheard the clerk. "My clerk—with such a small weekly income, and a wife and family— talking about a merry Christmas! Foolishness! Humbug!"

CHAPTER TWO

A Cold, Stingy Heart

As Scrooge's nephew was leaving, two other people came in. They were plump, pleasant-looking older gentlemen.

"Scrooge and Marley's, I believe," said one of the gentlemen. "Am I speaking to Mr. Scrooge, or Mr. Marley?"

"Mr. Marley has been dead for seven years," Scrooge replied. "He died on this very night, on Christmas Eve, seven years ago. What do you want from me?"

"At this joyful season of the year, Mr. Scrooge," said the gentleman, "we should think of others who are poor and have less than we have. There

are many families in this world who have no money, no food, no home, and no place to go to find comfort."

"Are there no prisons? Are there no poorhouses?" asked Scrooge.

"Plenty of them," said the gentleman, with a disappointed look. "Although I wish I could say there were not."

"Oh! I was afraid, from what you said at first, that they might have been closed down," said Scrooge. "I'm very glad to hear there are still places to send such people."

"We do not believe prisons and poorhouses provide much Christian cheer," replied the gentleman. "We are trying to collect some money to buy the Poor some food and clothing. We ask at Christmas time—a time when those of us who have Plenty should rejoice and share with those who have Need. How much do you wish to give?"

"Nothing!" said Scrooge. "I wish to be left alone. I don't make merry myself at Christmas, and I can't afford to make lazy people merry. I pay taxes to the government to support the prisons and poorhouses. These people you speak of can go there to find their Christmas cheer."

"Many *can't* go there," responded the gentleman, "and many would rather die."

"Fine," said Scrooge. "Let them die. The world has too many people anyhow. I have enough worries of my own. Good afternoon, gentlemen!"

Seeing that they could not change Scrooge's mind, the gentlemen left. Scrooge went back to his work feeling quite proud of himself.

Meanwhile, the fog and darkness thickened. People with torches offered to walk ahead of carriage horses and lead them on their way. The steeple of a church, whose gruff old bell was always peeping slyly down at Scrooge, was hidden from view. It struck the hours and quarter hours in the clouds, with trembling sounds, as if its teeth were chattering in its frozen head. The lamps in the shop windows along the main street shone like rosy smudges in the darkness.

It grew even foggier and colder—a piercing, biting cold. A shivering youngster bent down at the keyhole of Scrooge's door to sing him a Christmas carol. But at the first sound of his voice, Scrooge grabbed a ruler and moved angrily toward the door. The poor child ran away, scared to death of the mean old man.

When the time came to close the office for the day, Scrooge climbed down from his stool. The clerk in the next room quickly put his candle out, and put on his hat. Scrooge saw him.

"You'll want to be off work all day tomorrow, I suppose?" said Scrooge.

"If that would be quite all right, sir."

"It's not all right," said Scrooge, "and it's not fair. If I held back a day's pay for it, you'd think that was unfair to you, I am sure."

The clerk smiled faintly.

"And yet," said Scrooge, "you don't think it's unfair to *me*—when I pay for a day of no work."

"It *is* only once a year…"

"That's no excuse for picking a man's pocket every twenty-fifth of December!" said Scrooge, buttoning up his overcoat. "Well, I suppose you must have the whole day, but you be sure you get to work bright and early day after tomorrow!"

The clerk promised that he would. Scrooge closed the office and walked out with a growl. And the clerk, with the long ends of his white scarf flying out behind him, ran home to Camden Town as fast as he could to join his family in some Christmas Eve games.

After a lonely dinner by himself in a lonely tavern, Scrooge left for home. He lived in an apartment, which had once belonged to Marley. It was a gloomy set of rooms in a dark lump of a building up a side street. The building looked out of place, as if it must have run there when it was a young house, playing hide-and-seek with other houses, and forgotten the way out. It was old and lonely now, though, for nobody lived in it but Scrooge. All the other rooms were rented out as offices. The street was so dark that even Scrooge, who knew its every stone, had to feel his way along with his hands. The fog and frost hung thick around the door.

Now, it is a fact that there was nothing at all different about the knocker on the door, except that it was very large. It is also a fact that Scrooge had seen it, night and morning, the whole time he had lived in that place. Keep in mind, also, that Scrooge had not given one thought to Marley since speaking of his seven-years-dead partner that afternoon. So, explain to me, if you can, how it happened that, as he was putting his key in the door, Scrooge looked at the doorknocker and saw—*not* a knocker—but *Marley's face*!

Marley's face. It was not hidden in dark shadow as the other things around it were, but glowed with a dim, greenish light. It was not angry, but looked at Scrooge as Marley used to look, with ghostly spectacles turned up on its ghostly forehead. The hair fluttered strangely, as if blown by an invisible breeze. And though the eyes were wide open, they did not move.

CHAPTER THREE

Marley's Ghost

As Scrooge stared at this strange thing, it suddenly faded away and became a doorknocker again. Scrooge was scared and his blood ran cold, but he put his hand back on the key, turned it, walked inside, and lit his candle.

He *did* wait for a moment before he shut the door. And he *did* look cautiously behind it first, as if he thought he might see the back of Marley's head and pigtail sticking out into the hall. But there was nothing on the back of the door except the screws and nuts that held the knocker on.

"Phooey!" muttered Scrooge, and he closed the door with a bang.

The sound echoed like thunder through the rooms above and the cellars below. Scrooge locked the outside door, walked across the hall, and up the stairs—slowly, too, for his candle was small and the stairway was dark. Up Scrooge went, not caring a bit about that. Darkness is cheap, and Scrooge liked anything that was cheap. But before he shut his apartment door, he walked through his rooms to see that everything was all right, for he could not forget the memory of Marley's face on the door.

Living room, bedroom, storage room—all as they should be. Nobody under the table, nobody under the sofa. A small fire in the fireplace, and the little pot of tea on the warming shelf. Nobody under the bed, nobody in the closet, nobody in his nightshirt, which was hanging up against the wall. Nothing out of place in the storage room.

Feeling better, he closed his door and locked himself in—double-locked himself in—which he thought might protect him against any more surprises. He took off his scarf, put on his nightshirt, slippers, and nightcap, and sat down before the fire to have his tea.

As he sat there, an unused bell that hung in the room began mysteriously to swing. It swung so softly at first that it hardly made a sound. But soon it rang out loudly.

This might have lasted a minute, but it seemed like an hour. Then, just as it stopped, another frightening sound rang out—a strange clanking noise, deep down below, as if some person, or some *thing*, were dragging a heavy chain around in the cellar.

Suddenly, Scrooge heard the cellar door fly open with a booming sound. The clanking noise became much louder. Something was coming up the stairs—straight toward his door!

"It's humbug!" said Scrooge. "I won't believe it. I won't."

He changed his mind though, when something passed right through the locked door and into the room. As the thing entered, the dying flame in the fireplace leaped up, as though it were saying, "I know him! Marley's Ghost!" and fell again.

And it *was* Marley! Marley in his pigtail, wearing his usual coat, pants, and boots. A long chain was tied around his waist, and he dragged it behind him like a tail.

Scrooge looked closely at the chain, for it was made of moneyboxes, keys, padlocks, record books, deeds, and heavy safes made of steel. In a way, Marley seemed to have no body, for Scrooge could see right through the front of his coat to the two buttons on its back.

He could not believe his eyes! Though he saw the phantom standing before him—though he felt the chilling power of its death-cold eyes, and noticed the bandage wrapped around its head and chin—he still would not let himself believe what he saw.

"What's this!" said Scrooge, mean as ever. "What do you want with me?"

"Much!"—*It was Marley's voice, no doubt about it.*

"Who are you?"

"Ask me who I *was*."

"Who *were* you, then?" said Scrooge, raising his voice. "You're a bit fussy—for being nothing but a shadow."

"In life I was your partner—Jacob Marley. You don't look as though you believe in me."

"I don't," said Scrooge. "I say humbug! I do not believe in such nonsense!"

At this, the Spirit made such a frightful cry, and shook its chain with such an awful noise, that Scrooge held on tight to his chair to save himself from falling in a faint. His horror became even greater when the phantom took off the bandage from its head, and *its lower jaw dropped all the way down to its chest!*

Scrooge fell to his knees in shock.

"Mercy!" Scrooge begged. "Horrible phantom, why do you haunt me?"

"Man of the worldly mind!" replied the Ghost. "Will you believe in me or not?"

"I will," said Scrooge. "But why do spirits walk the earth, and why do they come to me?"

"The spirit of every man," the Ghost answered, "must walk among his fellow men, and travel far and wide. And if that spirit does not travel in life, it is condemned to do so after death. It has to wander through the world looking at sad things it can no longer change—things it might have changed when it lived, and turned to happiness!"

Again the phantom cried out and shook its long chain.

"You are tied in chains, like a prisoner," said Scrooge, trembling. "Tell me why."

"I *am* a prisoner—a prisoner of the chain I made for myself during my life," said the Ghost. "I made every inch of it. I chose to put it on, and I chose to wear it. Look at all the things it's made of. Are they strange to *you*? They should not be! They are the things of money and greed, and you are just as selfish and greedy as I was."

Scrooge trembled more and more.

"Do you not know the weight and length of the chain you yourself carry?" said the Ghost. "It was just as heavy and as long as this when I died, seven Christmas Eves ago. You have added more to it since then. Yours is a huge, heavy chain!"

Scrooge looked around him on the floor, expecting to find three or four hundred feet of iron chain, but he could see nothing.

"Jacob," Scrooge pleaded. "Old Jacob Marley, tell me more. Speak comfort to me, Jacob."

"I have none to give," the Ghost replied. "Comfort comes from other places, Ebenezer Scrooge. Comfort is given by other ministers, to other kinds of men. Nor can I tell you all that I would wish to tell you. I haven't much time. I cannot rest, I cannot stay long anywhere. My spirit never walked beyond our business office— Pay close attention to me!—When I was alive, my spirit never wandered beyond our greedy, money-grabbing office. And so, in death, I must travel far and wide."

"Seven years dead," said Scrooge. "And traveling all the time?"

"The whole time. No rest, no peace. Tortured the whole time by shame and sorrow."

"You travel fast?" asked Scrooge.

"On the wings of the wind," replied the Ghost.

"You should have been able to cover a lot of distance in seven years," said Scrooge.

"Oh! Not nearly enough distance!" the Ghost cried out. "As I told you, when I lived on this earth, I was bound by the chains of selfishness. The Christian spirit within me was trapped. I did not take the time in my short life to be kind and helpful to my fellow man. Now I travel the world over, paying for my mistakes. If only I had known then what I know now!"

"But you were always a good man of business, Jacob," said Scrooge, who now began to think about himself, and the way he led his own life.

"Business!" cried the Ghost. "*Mankind* should have been my business. Doing good for all people should have been my business. Charity, mercy, patience, and kindness should have been my business. The work at my office was nothing but a drop of water in the wide ocean of the *true* business of my life!"

It held up its chain, as if that were the cause of all its helpless sadness, and threw it heavily to the ground again.

"At this time of the year," the Spirit said, "I suffer most. Why did I walk through crowds of fellow human beings with my eyes turned down, and never raise them to the light of that blessed Star which led the Wise Men to a poor stable?— the light that would have led *me* to poor homes in need of comfort?"

Scrooge began to tremble even more.

"Listen to me!" cried the Ghost. "My time with you is nearly gone."

"I will," said Scrooge. "But don't be too hard on me, Jacob, I pray of you!"

"I have sat invisible beside you many, many days," said the Ghost. "That was just a small part of making up for the sins of my selfish life. But tonight you are allowed to see me so that I may warn you that you still have a chance and hope of avoiding what happened to me. I am here to give you that chance and hope, Ebenezer."

"You were always a good friend to me," said Scrooge. "Thank'ee!"

"You will be haunted," said the Ghost, "by Three Spirits."

Shocked by this, Scrooge's jaw dropped almost as low as the Ghost's had done earlier.

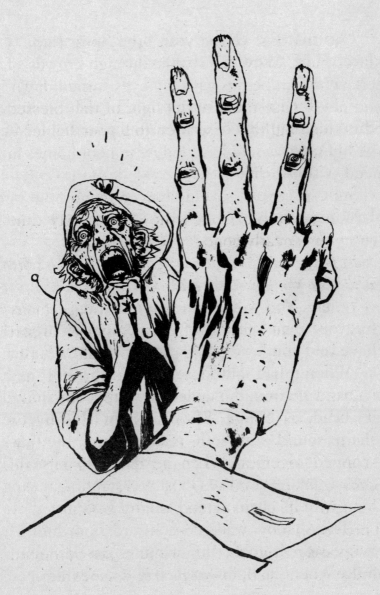

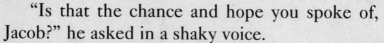

"Is that the chance and hope you spoke of, Jacob?" he asked in a shaky voice.

"It is."

"I—I think I'd rather not," said Scrooge, thinking that kind of chance might not be one he would enjoy.

"Without their visits," said the Ghost, "you cannot hope to avoid the path I walked. Listen carefully! *The first Spirit will visit tomorrow, when the bell strikes* ONE. *The second Spirit will come the next night at the same time—*ONE. *The third will visit you the night after that at the last stroke of* TWELVE. You will see me no more, but be sure, for your own sake, that you remember what I have told you."

When it had said these words, the Ghost took its bandage from the table and wrapped it around its head, as before. Scrooge knew this by the sharp sound its teeth made, when the jaws snapped together. When he dared to raise his eyes again, he saw the Ghost was standing, facing him, with its chain wound around its arm.

The shadow walked backward from him. At every step it took, the window raised itself a little. When the Spirit reached it, it was wide open.

Scrooge could hear strange sounds outside—
sounds of weeping and guilt. The Ghost listened,
then it joined in the sad sounds, floated out into
the dark night, and disappeared.

Scrooge ran to the window and looked out.

The air was filled with phantoms, wandering here and there, crying and moaning as they went. Every one of them wore chains like Marley's Ghost. None were free. One old ghost, with a huge iron safe fastened to its ankle, was crying sadly because he could not offer any help to a poor woman and her child. All the phantoms were suffering the same pain—they were trying to show human kindness and love, but had lost the power forever.

Suddenly these phantoms faded into mist and were gone.

Scrooge closed the window and checked the door through which the Ghost had entered. It was still double-locked—exactly as he had locked it with his own hands. He tried to say "Humbug!" but could not speak the word. He went straight to bed, without undressing, and fell asleep.

CHAPTER FOUR

The First Spirit—Young Scrooge

When Scrooge awoke, it was dark, and the bell in the church had just struck TWELVE.

Twelve? It was past two when he went to bed. So it must be twelve noon—but how could it still be dark? The clock must be wrong.

He checked his own clock, but its little chime struck TWELVE—and stopped.

"Why... is it possible," said Scrooge, "that I have slept through a whole day and far into another night? I must be dreaming."

Scrooge thought it over, and over, and could make no sense of it. The more he thought, the more confused he became.

43

As Scrooge lay there, he suddenly remembered that Marley's Ghost had warned him that the
first Spirit would visit when the bell struck ONE.
He decided to lie awake until the hour arrived.

Finally, the bell rang with a deep, hollow ONE.
Light flashed up in the room at that very instant,
and the curtains of his bed were suddenly pulled
back—*pulled back by a hand!* Scrooge found himself face-to-face with the ghostly visitor who had
opened the curtains.

It was a strange figure—like a child in some
ways, like an old man in others. Its hair, which
hung down its back, was white as if with old age,
but the face had not a wrinkle in it. Its robe was
pure white, tied at the waist by a sparkling,
shining belt. But the strangest thing about it was
that bright, clear rays of light seemed to burst
from the top of its head, lighting up the room.
The cap it held under its arm looked like a large
candle-snuffer, which it must have used to put
out the light.

"Are you the first Spirit, sir, that Marley said
would visit me?" asked Scrooge.

"I am."

The voice was soft and gentle—unusually low.

"Who, and what are you?" Scrooge asked.

"I am the Ghost of Christmas Past."

"*Long* Past?" asked Scrooge.

"No. *Your* past."

Scrooge did not know why, but he wanted to see the Spirit in his candle-snuffer cap, and begged him to put it on.

"What?" cried the Ghost. "Would you, with worldly hands, so soon put out the light I give? Is it not enough that you are one of those whose meanness and greed made this cap, and force me, year after year, to wear it?"

Scrooge said he had not meant to be rude, and that he had never purposely "capped" the Spirit at any time of his life. He then became bolder and asked why the Spirit had come.

"I am here for your own good," said the Ghost. "I am here to save you. Pay close attention! Rise! And walk with me!"

The Spirit's grip on Scrooge's arm, though gentle, was firm. He rose—but when the Spirit started to move toward the window, Scrooge pulled at its robe.

"I am human," Scrooge cried, "and I am likely to fall."

"Permit my hand to touch you *there*," said the Spirit, laying it over Scrooge's heart, "and I will lift you up and support you in more than this."

As the words were spoken, they passed right through the wall, and stood on an open country road, with fields on either side. The city had completely disappeared. The darkness and the mist had disappeared with it, for it was a clear, cold, winter day, with snow on the ground.

"Good Heavens!" said Scrooge, as he looked around. "I remember this place. I grew up here. I was a boy here!"

Boyhood memories filled Scrooge's mind and brought back thoughts of hopes, and joys, and cares long forgotten. The Spirit looked at him.

"Your lip is trembling," said the Ghost. "Is that a tear on your cheek?"

Scrooge muttered "Of course not," with lump in his throat, and begged the Ghost to lead him where it wished.

"Do you remember the way?" asked the Spirit.

"Remember it!" cried Scrooge. "I could walk it with my eyes closed."

"Strange that you had forgotten it for so many years!" said the Ghost. "Let us go on."

They walked along the road—Scrooge remembering every gate, and post, and tree—until a little market town appeared in the distance, with its bridge, its church, and winding river. Some shaggy ponies trotted toward them with boys on their backs, who called to other boys in country carriages and carts. All these boys were in a happy mood and shouted to each other. The crisp air was full of laughter.

"These are just shadows from your past," said the Ghost. "They do not know we are here."

As the happy travelers came nearer, Scrooge knew and named each of them. Why was he so happy and excited to see them? Why did his cold eye glisten, and his heart leap up as they went past? Why was he filled with gladness when he heard them wish each other Merry Christmas, as they left to go to their own homes? What was Merry Christmas to Scrooge? Merry Christmas? Nonsense! What good had it ever done him?

"The school where your father sent you to live is almost empty now," said the Ghost. "The children have gone home to be with their families at Christmas. Just one lonely child is left there, forgotten by his friends."

Scrooge said he knew it. And he sobbed.

They turned off the main road and came to a large building of dull red brick, with a school bell sitting on top.

Entering the building, the Ghost and Scrooge came upon a long, empty, gloomy room with rows of plain wooden benches and desks. At one of these desks a lonely boy was reading near a small fire. Scrooge sat down upon a bench and cried, for he saw that the boy was his own, poor forgotten self as he had used to be.

Every sight and sound softened Scrooge's heart and brought more tears to his eyes—the unseen echoes in the house, the squeak and scuffle of the mice behind the walls, and the clicking in the fire. They all brought back memories to Scrooge.

The Spirit touched him on the arm and pointed to the young Scrooge, still reading by the fire. Feeling sad and sorry for his earlier self, Scrooge said, "Poor boy!" and cried again.

"I wish…" Scrooge started to say, after drying his eyes with his coat sleeve. "But… but it's too late now."

"What is the matter?" asked the Spirit.

"Nothing," said Scrooge. "Nothing. There was a boy singing a Christmas carol at my door last night. I wish I had been kind and given him something. That's all."

The Ghost smiled thoughtfully and waved its hand, saying, "Let us see another Christmas from your past!"

As the Ghost spoke, Scrooge saw himself again, a little older now. But the boy he saw was not reading. He was walking back and forth, lonely and sad, in his small, dark room above the schoolroom. All the other boys had gone home to be with their families for the holidays, and young Scrooge was alone again.

Scrooge looked at the Ghost, and with a sad shaking of his head, looked toward the door of the boy's room.

It opened, and a girl, much younger than the boy, came running in. She put her arms around the boy, and kissed him, and called him her "Dear, dear brother."

"I have come to bring you home, dear brother!" said the child, clapping her tiny hands, and bending down to laugh. "To bring you home, home, home!"

"Home, Fannie?" cried the boy.

"Yes!" said the child, full of happiness. "Home, for good. Home, forever and ever. Father is so much kinder than he used to be, that home is like Heaven! He spoke so gently to me one night when I was going to bed, that I was not afraid to ask him once more if you might come home. He agreed that you should, and sent me in a coach to get you. And you'll never have to come back here. But first, we're to be together all Christmas long, and have the merriest time in all the world."

"You are quite a girl, little Fan!" said the boy.

She clapped her hands and laughed, and stood on tiptoe to hug him. Then she began to drag him, in her childish excitement, toward the door. And he, quite happily, went with her.

Just then, a terrible voice cried, "Bring down Master Scrooge's suitcase!" and in came the schoolmaster himself. He glared at young Master Scrooge with a cold, hard look. He shook hands with him, and wished him good-bye. After Master Scrooge's things had been tied onto the top of the coach, the children said good-bye to the schoolmaster very gladly, and rode happily down the snow-covered driveway.

"Your little sister was always a thin, weak girl," said the Ghost. "But she had a big heart."

"Yes, she did," cried Scrooge. "You're right about that!"

"She died a young woman," said the Ghost, "but, as I remember, she had children."

"Only one child," Scrooge said.

"True," said the Ghost. "Your nephew!"

Scrooge could say only "Yes," and no more, for he was thinking how unkind he had been when his nephew had visited his office.

CHAPTER FIVE

The First Spirit—At Fezziwig's

Just a few seconds later they had left the school behind them and were in the busy streets of a city. It was evening, and people hurried here and there. Scrooge could see by the decorations in the stores that it was Christmas time again.

The Ghost stopped at the door of a building, and asked Scrooge if he remembered it.

"Of course," said Scrooge. "This is where I lived and worked as an assistant to Mr. Fezziwig, while he trained me for my future work."

They went in. At the sight of an old gentleman in a wig, sitting behind a high desk, Scrooge cried in great excitement:

"Why, it's old Fezziwig! Bless his heart! It's Fezziwig alive again!"

Old Fezziwig laid down his pen and looked up at the clock. Laughing heartily, he called out in a kind warm, jolly voice:

"Yo ho, there! Ebenezer! Dick!"

Scrooge saw his past self, now a grown-up young man, come into the room, along with another of Mr. Fezziwig's assistants with whom he had worked.

"That's Dick Wilkins, to be sure," said Scrooge to the Ghost. "Bless me, yes. There he is. He was a good friend."

"Yo ho, my boys!" said Fezziwig, jumping down from his high desk. "No more work tonight. Christmas Eve, Dick! Christmas, Ebenezer! Put everything away, my lads, and let's have lots of room here! Hi-ho, Dick! Hi-ho, Ebenezer!"

It was done in a minute. Everything that could be moved was put away. The floor was swept and mopped, the lamp wicks were trimmed, and fuel was piled on the fire. And the office was as snug, and warm, and dry, and bright a ballroom as you would wish to see on a winter's night.

In came a fiddler. Sitting down at the high desk, he filled the whole room with music. In came Mrs. Fezziwig with one huge, kind smile. In came the three Miss Fezziwigs, smiling and lovable. In came all the young men and women who worked there. In came the housemaid, with her cousin, the baker. In came the cook, with her brother's best friend, the milkman. In came the boy from across the street, and the girl from two houses away. Kind old Fezziwig had invited them all. Soon, everyone was dancing. You never saw so much fun! Happy couples were everywhere.

There were more dances, and there were games. And there was cake, and Christmas punch, and great pieces of cold meat, and there were mince pies.

But the great moment of the evening came after the food and games, when the fiddler started to play old Fezziwig's favorite tune. Up he got to dance with Mrs. Fezziwig. Oh, how they could dance! Before long, they were leading twenty or more couples around the floor, twirling, spinning, swinging, and bowing. What a dance! What a good time!

When the clock struck ELEVEN, the party ended. Mr. and Mrs. Fezziwig stood on either side of the door, wishing everyone Merry Christmas as they left. When everybody had gone except young Ebenezer Scrooge and Dick, they wished them Merry Christmas, and the two lads turned to leave for their beds in the back shop.

As he stood with the Ghost, Scrooge had watched the scene with excitement. His heart and soul were in it as he saw himself as a younger man. He remembered everything, enjoyed everything, and felt strangely disturbed by it all. Then he remembered the Ghost, and saw that it was looking straight at him, while the light from its head shone brightly.

"It seems silly," said the Ghost, "for these people to be so happy, just because Fezziwig had a little party for them."

"Silly? Why is it silly?" asked Scrooge.

"He has spent very little worldly money on them. Should he get so much praise for so little money spent?"

"It isn't that," said Scrooge, a little angry by what the Ghost had said, and speaking more like the young Ebenezer than his older, meaner self.

"It isn't that, Spirit. He has the power to make us happy or unhappy, to make our work light or heavy, pleasant or unpleasant. His kindness to those who work for him cost him nothing, but it is a greater gift than all the money in the world."

He felt the Spirit staring at him, and stopped.

"What is the matter?" asked the Ghost.

"Nothing. I was just thinking, that's all," said Scrooge quietly.

"Thinking about what? What is on your mind?" the Ghost insisted.

"I was wishing to myself that I could speak a kind word or two to my clerk just now, that's all."

As he spoke, Fezziwig's offices faded away and disappeared, and Scrooge and the Ghost again stood side by side in the open air.

"I don't have much time," said the Spirit. "We must go! Quick!"

CHAPTER SIX

The First Spirit—A Light Goes Out

Suddenly, they were once more in a different place. Again Scrooge saw a scene from his past. It was a few years after the party at Fezziwig's, and Scrooge saw himself sitting with a pretty young girl named Belle, whom he had once loved and been engaged to marry.

There were tears in the girl's eyes, which sparkled in the light that shone out of the head of the Ghost of Christmas Past.

She was saying softly, "You have come to love something more than me. Something has taken my place in your heart. But if it will make your life happy, I have no reason to be sad."

"What has taken your place?" Scrooge heard his younger self ask.

"A golden Idol. Money!" she answered. "You have given up all of your good hopes and dreams. Money and Profit have become the only things you care about."

"So what?" he said. "Even if I have grown so much wiser, what difference does that make? I am not changed toward you."

"You *are* changed! When we fell in love, and were poor, we said that we would improve our lives by patient, hard work. When we agreed to that, you were a different man. Things that once made us happy now bring sadness. I have thought a lot about this, and I can let you go."

"Have I ever asked you to let me go?"

"In words, no. Never. But tell me, if we had never before met and fallen in love," said Belle, "would you try to win my love now? Would you choose a *poor* girl, now that money is all you care about? I don't think so. And even if you did, I think you would wish you had not."

He seemed to feel she was probably right, though he didn't like to admit it to himself. The girl went on speaking.

"If my words make you sad, perhaps you are thinking of old memories. In a way, I hope your memories do make you sad. But you will soon forget me and go back to your Idol of Money. I could never make you as happy as Money will make you. I hope you are happy in the life you have chosen."

She left him, and they parted.

"Spirit," said Scrooge, "show me no more! Take me home. Why do you enjoy torturing me?"

"One shadow more! You must see one more thing from your past," said the Ghost.

"No more!" cried Scrooge. "No more. I don't wish to see it. Show me no more!"

But the Ghost would not listen to him, and forced him to watch what happened next.

They were in another room, not very large or fancy, but full of comfort. Scrooge saw Belle, now grown older, sitting next to the winter fire. She was laughing happily with her beautiful daughter, who looked exactly as Belle had looked when Scrooge had first met her.

The door opened. The daughter rushed to greet her father whose arms were loaded down with Christmas presents.

Oh, the shouts of joy and wonder when she saw him, and the happiness and thanks when the packages were passed out. Oh, how she hugged that man! Finally, when the excitement was over, the three sat down together at the fireside.

Now Scrooge watched more carefully than ever, and saw how lovingly the daughter rested her head on her father's shoulder. When Scrooge thought that he might have had a daughter like that, who would have brought him joy in his old age, his eyes filled with tears. As he watched, the father spoke.

"Belle," he said, turning to his wife with a smile, "I saw an old friend of yours this afternoon."

"Who was it?"

"Mr. Scrooge. I passed his office window, and could not help seeing him. His partner, Jacob Marley, is near death, I hear. And there he sat alone. All alone in the world, I do believe."

"Spirit!" cried Scrooge to the Ghost, "take me away from here."

"I told you these were shadows of *your* own past," said the Ghost. "Do not blame *me* for what you see."

"Take me away!" Scrooge cried. "I cannot stand to watch it!"

He turned on the Ghost, and began to wrestle with it, saying, "Leave me! Show me no more of my past. Haunt me no longer!"

As he struggled with the Ghost, Scrooge saw that the light from its head burned high and bright. He grabbed the Ghost's cap and pressed it down on its head, hoping the light would go out.

The Spirit dropped beneath it, so that the cap covered its whole form. Scrooge pressed it down with all his strength, but he could not hide the light, which flooded out from under it along the ground.

Suddenly Scrooge felt tired and sleepy, and saw that he was back in his own bedroom. He gave the Ghost's cap one last squeeze and stumbled to his bed, where he fell into a deep sleep.

CHAPTER SEVEN

The Second Spirit—The Torch

Scrooge awoke in the middle of a huge snore and sat up in bed to get his thoughts together. He was sure it must be almost ONE, the time Marley had told him the second Ghost would visit him. He pulled his bed curtains back, and lying down again, kept a sharp lookout so this second Spirit would not surprise him.

But he *was* surprised—surprised that when the church bell rang ONE, no Ghost appeared. Five, ten, fifteen minutes went by, and still he saw no phantom. The only thing he noticed was that a bright light seemed to be shining on his bed. This scared him more than a dozen ghosts because he did not know what it meant. He trembled with fear. The light seemed to be coming from the next room. He got up and moved quietly to the door.

The moment Scrooge's hand was on the door-knob, a strange voice called him by his name, and invited him to enter. He obeyed.

He walked into his own living room—but it was changed. It seemed to be full of Christmas cheer. Holly, red berries, mistletoe, and ivy were hanging from the walls and ceiling. There was a roaring fire in the fireplace. It was a larger fire than that room had ever known in all the time Scrooge had lived there. Piled up on the floor, in the shape of a throne, were wonderful foods of every kind. There were turkeys, geese, chickens, roasts of beef, sausages, pies, chestnuts, apples, oranges, cherries, pears, large cakes, puddings, and bowls of hot, bubbling Christmas punch.

Relaxing upon this throne was a jolly Giant, who held a glowing torch up high to shine its light on Scrooge as he came peeping around the door. It seemed to Scrooge, though he didn't understand why, as if all the peaceful cheer and rich blessings in the room had somehow been poured out of that torch.

"Come in!" said the Ghost. "Come in and get to know me better, man!"

Scrooge entered quietly and carefully, and hung his head before this Spirit. He was not the bold, forceful Scrooge he had been. Though the Spirit's eyes were clear and kind, he did not like to look straight into them.

"I am the Ghost of Christmas Present," said the Spirit. "Look at me!"

Scrooge did so, and saw that it was dressed in a simple green robe, trimmed with white fur. On its head it wore a holly wreath, decorated with shining icicles. Its dark brown curly hair hung free—free as its friendly face, its sparkling eye, its open hand, its cheery voice, and its relaxed, joyful manner. It wore a belt around its waist, but there was no sword in the belt. Instead of a weapon of death, this new Spirit carried only its bright torch of life.

"You have never seen anything like me before!" exclaimed the Spirit.

"Never," Scrooge answered.

"Have you never walked with other members of my family, brothers of mine, who have come in years past?" the Spirit asked.

"I don't think I have," said Scrooge. "No. I am afraid I have not. But have you had many brothers, Spirit?"

"Hundreds and hundreds—one for every year since the very first Christmas," said the Ghost.

"A huge family to feed," muttered stingy Scrooge, thinking only of the cost.

The Ghost of Christmas Present stood up.

"Spirit," said Scrooge humbly, "lead me where you wish. I was forced to go out last night against my will, and I learned a lesson which I have not forgotten. Tonight, if you have anything at all to teach me, let me gain something from it."

"Touch my robe!" said the Spirit.

Scrooge did as he was told.

In a flash, the fire, the room, and all of the wonderful things in it magically disappeared. Even the night itself was gone, and now they stood in the city streets on a snowy Christmas morning. The people were busy scraping snow from sidewalks and the tops of their houses.

The sky was gloomy, and the streets were choked up with a grimy, foggy mist, yet there was a feeling of cheerfulness in all the people, who greeted each other with warm holiday smiles.

Even those who were shoveling away on the housetops were merry. They called out to one another, and now and then they threw a friendly snowball.

But soon the steeple bells called all good people to church. Out they came, in their best clothes, and with their happiest faces. And at the same time there appeared, from dozens of side streets and alleys, great numbers of poorer people, people who had no ovens of their own at home. They were carrying their dinners to be cooked at the bakers' shops.

These poor people seemed to interest the Ghost more than the others. It stood, with Scrooge beside it, in a baker's doorway and sprinkled their dinners with something from its torch as they passed by. It was a very strange kind of torch. Once or twice when there were angry words between some people who had bumped into each other, the Ghost shook a few drops on them from it, and their friendliness quickly returned. For, they said, it was a shame to quarrel on Christmas Day. And so it was! God love it, so it was!

"Is there a special flavor in what you sprinkle from your torch?" Scrooge asked the Spirit.

"There is. It is my own."

"Would it work on any kind of dinner on this day?" asked Scrooge.

"To any dinner kindly given. To a poor one most of all."

"Why to a poor one most?" asked Scrooge.

"Because it is the one that needs it most. Now come, we must travel on."

CHAPTER EIGHT

The Second Spirit—The Cratchits

They went on, invisible, straight to the home of Scrooge's clerk. On the doorstep the Spirit smiled, and stopped to bless Bob Cratchit's small, four-roomed house with the sprinkling of its torch. Think of that! Bob, who earned so little and was so poor, and yet the Ghost of Christmas Present blessed his home! Then the Spirit and Scrooge stopped to watch and listen.

Bob Cratchit's wife, dressed in an old, patched gown, was setting the table. Belinda Cratchit, her second daughter, was helping her, while her oldest son, Master Peter Cratchit, stuck a fork into the saucepan of potatoes.

Then, two smaller Cratchits, boy and girl, came tearing in, screaming that outside the baker's they had smelled the goose cooking, and known it must have been their own. Filled with happy thoughts of the tasty meal, these young Cratchits danced around the table and praised their older brother, Peter, while he blew the fire until the potatoes, bubbling up, knocked loudly at the saucepan lid to be let out and peeled.

"Where is your dear father, then?" said Mrs. Cratchit. "And your brother, Tiny Tim? And your older sister, Martha? She wasn't this late last Christmas Day."

"Here's Martha, Mother!" said a girl, coming in the door as she spoke.

"Here's Martha, Mother!" cried the two young Cratchits. "Hurrah! There's *such* a wonderful goose cooking, Martha!"

"Why, bless your heart alive, my dear, how late you are!" said Mrs. Cratchit, kissing her a dozen times, and excitedly taking off her coat and hat for her.

"We had a lot of work to finish up last night," replied the girl, "and had to put things away this morning, Mother."

"Well! Never mind so long as you are here," said Mrs. Cratchit. "Sit ye down by the fire, my dear, and warm yourself. Lord bless ye!"

"No, no! There's Father coming!" cried the two young Cratchits, who were everywhere at once. "Hide, Martha, hide!"

So Martha hid herself, and in came the father, with at least three feet of scarf hanging down in front of him, and his ragged clothes sewn up for the holidays. Tiny Tim was on his shoulders. Sadly for Tiny Tim, he carried a little crutch, and on his crippled legs he wore an iron brace.

"Why, where's our Martha?" cried Bob Cratchit, looking around.

"Not coming," said Mrs. Cratchit.

"Not coming?" said Bob, clearly very sad, after hurrying home all the way from church with Tim on his shoulders. "Martha not coming on Christmas Day?"

Martha didn't like to see him unhappy, even if it were only in fun, so she came out from behind the closet door, and ran into his arms. The two young Cratchits carried Tiny Tim off into the kitchen, so he could hear the pudding singing in the pan.

"And how did little Tim behave?" asked Mrs. Cratchit, after she had teased Bob about being fooled by Martha, and Bob had given his daughter a big hug.

"As good as gold," said Bob, "and better. Somehow he thinks a lot, sitting by himself so much, and says the strangest things you ever heard. He told me, coming home, that he hoped the people saw him in the church, because he was a cripple, and it might be pleasant to them to remember, on Christmas Day, the One who made lame beggars walk and blind men see."

Bob's voice trembled when he told them this, and shook even more when he said that Tiny Tim was growing stronger.

His little crutch was heard on the floor, and back came Tiny Tim, led by his brother and sister to his stool in front of the fire. Bob stirred up a jug of punch and put it on the fireplace shelf to warm, while Master Peter and the two young Cratchits went to the baker's to pick up the goose. They soon returned, holding it up and marching proudly, as if they were leading a grand parade. Tiny Tim gave a loud cheer for the goose, and the Cratchits gathered round the table.

The grace was said, and the Cratchit family had a wonderful Christmas dinner together. There never *was* such a goose! Bob said he didn't believe there ever was such a goose *cooked*. Along with the applesauce and mashed potatoes, it was plenty of dinner for the whole family, especially the youngest Cratchits, who were filled with goose up to the eyebrows! Then, as Miss Belinda put the dessert plates on the table, Mrs. Cratchit left the room. In half a minute she came back, smiling proudly, with the pudding.

Oh, a wonderful pudding! Bob Cratchit said that he thought it was the best pudding Mrs. Cratchit had ever made. Everybody had something to say about it, but nobody said or thought it was too small a pudding for a large family. The Cratchit family never complained and were always thankful for what they had.

At last the dinner was all done. The table was cleared, and more wood was added to the fireplace. Apples and oranges were put on the table, and a shovel-full of chestnuts was placed on the fire. The whole family gathered around in a circle. Bob served the hot punch, lifted his cup, and gave a toast.

"A Merry Christmas to us all, my dears. God bless us!"

"Merry Christmas and God bless us!" said the rest of the Cratchits.

"God bless us, every one!" said little Tiny Tim, the last of all.

He sat very close to his father's side on his little stool. Bob lovingly held his little hand in his, as if he feared terribly that his little boy might be taken from him.

"Spirit," said Scrooge, with a heartfelt interest and worry he had never felt before, "tell me if Tiny Tim will live."

"I see an empty little chair in the corner by the fireplace," replied the Ghost, "and a lonely crutch without an owner, carefully kept there in his memory. If these shadows remain unchanged by the Future, the child will die."

"No, no," said Scrooge. "Oh, no, kind Spirit! Tell me he will live!"

"If these shadows remain unchanged by the Future, this is the last Christmas we will find him here," returned the Ghost. "But, what does it matter if he dies? After all: *The world has too many people anyhow.*"

Scrooge hung his head to hear his own words repeated back to him by the Spirit. He was filled with guilt and sadness.

"Man," said the Ghost, "if you *are* a man, and your heart is not made of stone, forget that wicked thought, stop speaking such evil words. Who are you to say which men shall live, which men shall die? It may be that in the sight of Heaven *you* are more worthless and deserve more to die than millions like this poor man's child. O God! How can a man whose stomach is full be so cold and unkind toward those whose stomachs are empty?"

The Ghost's sharp words made Scrooge bend forward in shame. Trembling, he bowed his head and stared at the ground. But he looked up quickly when he heard his own name. Bob Cratchit was speaking.

"To Mr. Scrooge!" said Bob. "I'll give a toast to Mr. Scrooge, the one who pays my wages, the Source of the Feast! To his health!"

"The Source of the Feast indeed!" cried Mrs. Cratchit angrily. "I wish I had him here. I'd give him a piece of my mind to feast upon, and I hope he'd have a good appetite for it."

"My dear," said Bob, "don't say such things in front of the children! It's Christmas Day."

"It should be Christmas Day, I am sure," said Mrs. Cratchit. "One could only drink to the health of such a hateful, stingy, uncaring man as Mr. Scrooge on Christmas Day. You know he is hateful and stingy, Bob. Nobody knows that better than you do, poor fellow."

"My dear," said Bob calmly, "please. It's Christmas Day."

"I'll drink to his health for your sake and the sake of Christmas Day," said Mrs. Cratchit, "but not for his sake. Long life to him! A Merry Christmas and a Happy New Year. He'll be very merry and very happy, I am sure!"

The rest of the family joined in. Happy to have the thought of Scrooge behind them, they were ten times merrier than before. The chestnuts and the punch were passed around. After a while, Tiny Tim sang a song about a lost child traveling in the snow. He had a soft, sad little voice, just perfect for the song.

There was nothing so special about all this. They were not a rich, fancy family. They were not well dressed. There were holes in their shoes.

Their clothes were old and worn. But they were happy and thankful for the good time they had shared. And when they began to fade away and disappear, made even happier by the bright sprinklings of the Spirit's torch as they parted, Scrooge kept his eye on them, and especially on Tiny Tim, until the very last.

And then they were gone.

CHAPTER NINE

The Second Spirit—Nephew Fred

By this time it was getting dark, and snowing pretty heavily. As Scrooge and the Spirit went along the streets, the happiness of Christmas was all around them. There were warm fires in the cozy homes, dinners being cooked, children running to the door to greet their relatives who had come to visit. How the Ghost rejoiced! It stretched out its hand as it floated on, pouring bright gladness on everything it passed.

On and on they flew. The Ghost led Scrooge away from the city and into every corner of the earth—to the huts of poor miners, to a lonely lighthouse, to ships on dark and stormy seas.

In each place, Scrooge saw happy people being kind to one another, full of the love of Christmas and blessed by the Spirit with whom he traveled.

Just as Scrooge had begun to think these wild journeys to far-off places would never end, he was suddenly shocked and surprised to hear laughter and a voice he knew. Though he could not explain how, Scrooge found himself in a bright room, with the Spirit standing smiling by his side and looking with warmth and friendliness at—whom do you think?—Scrooge's own nephew!

"Ha, ha!" laughed the nephew. "Ha, ha, ha!"

You have never heard a finer laugh! And his laughter made everyone else laugh with him, as it spread through the room. Soon his nephew's wife (Scrooge's niece by marriage) and all the family and friends gathered there joined in.

"Ha, ha! Ha, ha, ha, ha!"

"He said Christmas was a humbug, He did!" cried Scrooge's nephew. "He believed it, too!"

"Shame upon him, Fred!" said his pretty wife.

"He's an odd old man," said Scrooge's nephew, "that's the truth—and not too pleasant. However, his sins carry their own punishment, and I have nothing to say against him."

"I'm sure he is very rich, Fred," said Scrooge's niece. "At least you always tell *me* so."

"So what, my dear?" said Scrooge's nephew. "His money is of no use to him. He don't do any good with it. He don't make himself comfortable with it. He don't even have the pleasure of thinking—ha, ha, ha!—that he is ever going to give *us* some of it."

"I have no patience with him," said his wife.

Her two sisters, and all the other ladies in the room, said the same thing.

"Oh, I have!" said Scrooge's nephew. "I am sorry for him. I couldn't be angry with him if I tried. Who suffers by his bad moods? He does, always. Here, he makes up his mind to dislike us, and he won't come and eat with us. What's the result? He misses out on the fine dinner we've just had and loses some pleasant moments— much pleasanter than those he can find in his moldy old office, or his dusty apartment. I plan to give him the same chance every year, whether he likes it or not, for I pity him. He may be bitter at Christmas till he dies, but he can't help thinking about it if I keep going, in good spirits, year after year, and saying, 'Uncle Scrooge, how are you?'

If it only puts him in the mood to give his poor clerk a little something extra at Christmas, that's something. And I think I shook him up yesterday when I invited him to have dinner with us and told him what *I* thought about Christmas. Ha, ha!"

After the rest had a good laugh at this, they all gathered around to have some music. They were a musical family. They knew what they were doing when it came to singing harmony, I promise you—especially Topper, a bachelor who had his eye on the plump sister of Scrooge's niece. He could growl out a good bass part, and never get red in the face over it.

Scrooge's niece played well upon the harp. She played a simple little song which Scrooge remembered had been a favorite of his sister, Fan. Little Fan, thought Scrooge, who, long ago, had come at Christmas time to take him home from his lonely school, as the Ghost of Christmas Past had reminded him. At the very first notes of that tune, all the things the first Ghost had shown him came back into his mind. His heart softened more and more, and he thought that if he could have listened to that sweet tune more often, years ago, he might have been a kinder, happier man.

But the nephew's family and friends didn't spend the whole evening singing. After a while they played a few simple games. For it is good to be children sometimes, especially at Christmas, when the mighty Creator was a child himself.

There was a game called "Yes and No," where Scrooge's nephew had to think of something, and the rest had to guess what it was by asking "yes or no" questions. After the first few questions, everyone knew he was thinking of an animal, a live animal, a disagreeable animal, a mean animal, an animal that growled and grunted sometimes, and talked sometimes, and lived in London, and walked around the streets, and wasn't in a circus, and wasn't led around by anybody, and didn't live in a zoo, and was not a horse, or a donkey, or a cow, or a bull, or a tiger, or a dog, or a pig, or a cat, or a bear. At every new question that was asked of him, the nephew burst into a fresh roar of laughter. At last the plump sister, just as amused, cried out:

"I have figured it out! I know what it is, Fred! I know what it is!"

"What is it?" cried Fred.

"It's your Uncle Scro-o-o-oge!"

And she was right. Everyone said it had been a good game, though some said the answer to "Is it a bear?" should have been "Yes," instead of "No," since they would have guessed right away that it was Mr. Scrooge. This brought more laughter.

"He has given us plenty to laugh about, I am sure," said Fred. "For that, we should be thankful and drink to his health. Lift your glasses and join me in a toast. I say, 'Here's to Uncle Scrooge!' "

"To Uncle Scrooge!" the others cried.

"A Merry Christmas and a Happy New Year to the old man, whatever kind of animal he is," said Fred. "He wouldn't accept it from me, but may he have it, anyhow. Here's to Uncle Scrooge!"

As he stood with the Spirit watching all this, Scrooge had become so merry that he would have given an invisible toast of his own, if the Ghost had given him time. But the whole scene passed away in the breath of the last word spoken by his nephew, and Scrooge and the Spirit were again off on their journeys.

They traveled far and visited many homes. The Spirit stood beside sick people, and they became cheerful. It sprinkled its blessings on poor people, and they felt rich. It visited families in far-off countries, and they felt closer to home. Everywhere it went, people were given new hope. In poorhouse, hospital, and jail, and every other place where there was suffering, as long as foolish, worldly Man had not closed the door and locked the Spirit out, it left its blessing. At every place, Scrooge learned more and more about the true meaning of Christmas.

It was a long night, and a strange night. Strange because, while Scrooge remained un- changed in his looks, the Ghost grew older, clearly older. Scrooge had been watching this change and now spoke of it when he saw that its hair had turned gray.

"Are spirits' lives so short?" asked Scrooge.

"My life upon this earth is very short," said the Ghost. "It ends tonight."

"Tonight!" cried Scrooge.

"Tonight at midnight. I have only a few more minutes with you."

"Forgive me for asking," said Scrooge, looking hard at the Spirit's robe, "but I see something strange sticking out from under your robe. Is it a foot or a claw?"

"It could be a claw, as little flesh as there is on it," was the Spirit's sad reply. "Look here."

From under its robe, it brought two children— hopeless, frightful, horrible, starving—nothing but skin and bones. They knelt down at its feet and clung to the outside of its clothing.

"Oh, Man! Look here! Look, look down here!" cried the Ghost.

They were a boy and a girl—skinny and ragged—their faces pinched and twisted. They were like small monsters, twice as horrible as had ever been created.

Scrooge stepped back, shocked.

"Spirit, are they... are they yours?" Scrooge could say no more.

"No. They are Man's. They are children of *your* world, not mine!" said the Spirit, looking down at them. "This boy is Ignorance. This girl is Poverty. Beware them both, but most of all beware this boy."

"Have they no shelter or support? No place to go? No one to help them?" cried Scrooge.

"*Are there no prisons? Are there no poorhouses?*" said the Spirit, repeating the exact words Scrooge had used when he had refused to give anything to the two gentlemen who had visited him in his office on Christmas Eve.

As Scrooge stood wishing that he had never spoken such mean words, he heard a clock somewhere striking TWELVE.

Scrooge looked around for the Ghost of Christmas Present, but it was gone.

CHAPTER TEN

The Third Spirit—The Merchants

As the last stroke of the bell faded away, Scrooge remembered that old Jacob Marley had said that the third Ghost would come at exactly that time. Lifting up his eyes, he saw a dark Phantom, shrouded and hooded, coming toward him, like a mist along the ground.

The Phantom slowly, silently came nearer and nearer to Scrooge. It seemed to fill the air with gloom and mystery.

It was covered in a black cloak, which hid its head, its face, and its shape. It held out one outstretched hand. The Spirit did not speak or move. Scrooge was filled with a dark fear.

"You must be the Ghost of Christmas Yet To Come, the Ghost of the Future?" said Scrooge.

The Spirit did not answer, but pointed onward with its hand.

"You are going to show me shadows of the things that have not yet happened, but will happen in the future," Scrooge went on. "Is that true, Spirit?"

The upper part of the cloak moved for an instant, as if the Spirit had nodded its head. That was the only answer it gave.

Although Scrooge was quite used to ghosts by this time, he feared the silent shape so much that his legs trembled beneath him. He found that he could hardly stand when he tried to follow it. The Spirit waited a moment, as if it saw his problem. This scared Scrooge even more, knowing that behind the dark shroud there were ghostly eyes watching him.

"Ghost of the Future!" he cried. "I fear you more than any phantom I have seen. But since I know you are here to do me good, and since I hope to live to be a different man from what I was, I am prepared to follow you, and do it with a thankful heart. Will you not speak to me?"

It did not answer. The hand was pointed straight ahead of them.

"Lead on!" said Scrooge. "Lead on! The night is fading fast, and I know it is precious time to me. Lead on, Spirit!"

The Phantom moved away in the same silent way it had approached. Scrooge followed in its shadow, which supported him, he thought, and carried him along.

Suddenly they came into the middle of the city's business district. There they saw merchants, who hurried up and down, and clinked the money in their pockets, and talked in groups, and looked at their watches, as Scrooge had seen them do so often.

The Spirit stopped beside one little group of businessmen. Seeing that the Spirit's hand was pointed toward them, Scrooge moved closer to listen to what they were saying.

"No," said a fat man, "I don't know much about it, either way. I only know he's dead."

"When did he die?" asked another.

"Last night, I believe."

"Why, what was the matter with him?" asked a third man. "I thought he'd never die."

"God knows," said the first, with a yawn, as if he didn't really care much about it.

"What has he done with his money?" asked a red-faced gentleman.

"I haven't heard," said the fat man, yawning again. "Left it to his Company, perhaps. He hasn't left it to *me*. That's all I know."

This made all the men laugh.

"It will probably be a very cheap funeral," said the same man. "For I swear I don't know of anybody who will go to it. Should we make up a group and volunteer?"

"I don't mind going if a lunch is provided," said the red-faced gentleman. "If I attend a funeral, I must be fed."

Another laugh.

"Well," said the first speaker, "I never eat lunch, but I'll go, if anybody else will. Bye-bye!"

The men walked away. Scrooge did not understand what he had heard, and looked to the Spirit for an answer. But it said nothing.

The Phantom glided on. Its finger pointed to two men Scrooge knew well. He listened again, hoping to understand why the Ghost was showing him these things.

"How are you?" said one.

"How are you?" replied the other.

"Well!" said the first. "He's dead. The Devil has got his own at last, hey?"

"So I am told," returned the second. "Cold weather, isn't it?"

"About right for Christmas time. You're not a skater, I suppose?"

"No. No. Things to do. Good morning to you!"

Not another word. That was all they had to say about a man's death, whoever he was.

Scrooge was confused. Why had the Spirit shown him these men? What was important about what they had said? There must be *some* hidden meaning, but what could it be? They couldn't have been talking about the death of Jacob, his old partner, for that was in the Past, and this Ghost was showing him the Future. No matter what it meant or who it was that might have died, it must have some important lesson. He decided to remember every word he heard, and everything he saw. He would especially watch the shadow of *himself* when it appeared. For he was sure that the actions of his future self would give him clues and help him solve the puzzle.

He looked around among the businessmen, hoping to see himself. It was, after all, the time of day when Scrooge was usually with the merchants, discussing deals. But some other man was standing where Scrooge had usually stood. He did not see himself among the crowds. He was not surprised, however. He had already begun to think that he needed to make some changes in his life. He thought and hoped that in this look into his future, he might be seeing some of the changes that had taken place.

Quiet and dark, the Ghost still stood beside him, with its outstretched hand. Scrooge felt as though its hidden eyes were staring straight at him. It made him shiver.

CHAPTER ELEVEN

The Third Ghost—The Thieves

They left the busy scene and went into a bad, rundown part of the town. The streets were dark and narrow, the shops and houses were falling apart, and the people were dirty and half-dressed. Crime and misery were everywhere.

Deep in this terrible neighborhood, there was a low, slope-roofed shack. Inside the shack Scrooge saw scrap iron, old rags, bottles, bones, and any kind of garbage you can think of, all piled up. There among the trash was the man who bought and sold this junk. He was a sly, gray-haired rascal, nearly seventy years old. He sat calmly smoking his pipe.

Just as Scrooge and the Ghost came upon this man, a woman with a heavy bag was sneaking into the shop. She had only just entered when another woman, also carrying a bag, came in, followed closely behind by a man in black clothing. All three of them were at first startled to see each other, but soon they all burst out laughing. By this time, the old man with the pipe had joined them.

"Let the old man's cleaning woman be the first in line!" cried the woman who had entered first. "Let his laundry woman be the second. And let the undertaker's man who worked on the body be the third. Look here, old Joe, here's a coincidence! We've all three met here without meaning to!"

"You couldn't have met in a better place," said old Joe, removing his pipe from his mouth. "Come into the parlor. Ain't none of you strangers, you know. Ha, ha! Come into the parlor. We're all of us pretty much alike. Ha, Ha!"

The "parlor" was the space behind a screen of rags. The old man stirred the fire with the leg of an old chair. He trimmed his smoky lamp (for it was night) with the stem of his pipe, and then put the pipe in his mouth again.

While he did this, the laundry woman threw her bag on the floor, and sat down on a stool. She looked boldly at the other two.

"Why do you look at me so odd, Mrs. Dilber?" said the cleaning woman. "Every person has a right to take care of themselves. *He* always did!"

"Well, that's true enough!" said the laundry woman. "No man watched out for himself more than him. No man was more selfish."

"Well, then, don't stand staring as if you was afraid, woman. Who's ever going to know? We're not going to tell on each other, I suppose?"

"No, indeed!" said Mrs. Dilber and the man together. "We should hope not."

"Very well, then!" cried the cleaning woman. "That's enough. Who's going to miss a few things like these? Not a *dead* man, I guess."

"No, indeed," said Mrs. Dilber, laughing.

"If that greedy old man had wanted to keep 'em after he was dead," said the cleaning woman, "why wasn't he different when he was alive? If he had been, he'd have had somebody to take care of him when he was struck with Death. Instead, he just lay there gasping out his last breath, alone by himself."

"It's the truest word that ever was spoke," said Mrs. Dilber. "He brought it on himself. It's his own fault. It's a judgment on him."

"Right you are," replied the cleaning woman. "Open that bag, old Joe, and let me know what you'll pay for it. Speak out plain and clear. I'm not afraid to go first, nor afraid for them to see it. We know pretty well that we were helping ourselves to a few of the old man's things before we met here. It's no sin. Open the bag, Joe."

But the man in black would not allow this. Bravely stepping forward, he took out his loot first. It was not much—a pencil-case, a pair of sleeve buttons, and a cheap pin. Old Joe looked them over and wrote the amounts he was willing to pay for them on the wall.

"That's your total," said Joe. "And I wouldn't offer a penny more, if I was to be boiled for not doing it. Who's next?"

Mrs. Dilber was next. She took out some sheets and towels, a few clothes, two silver teaspoons, and a few boots. Old Joe wrote what he would pay for them on the wall, in the same way as before.

"And now, you'll open *my* bag, Joe," said the cleaning woman.

Joe untied a great many knots and pulled out a large, heavy roll of some dark stuff.

"What is this?" said Joe. "Bed curtains?"

"Right you are, Joe," she said, laughing. "Bed curtains!"

"You don't mean to say you took 'em down, rings and all, with him lying there in his bed?" said Joe.

"Yes, I do," replied the woman. "Why not?"

"You were born to make your fortune," said Joe, "and you'll certainly do it."

"I certainly won't hold back my hand when I can reach out and take something, especially if I'm taking it from a man like *him*, I promise you, Joe," said the woman coolly. "Don't spill that lamp oil on those blankets, now."

"*His* blankets?" asked Joe.

"Whose else's do you think?" replied the woman. "He ain't likely to catch a cold without 'em, I'd bet."

"I hope he didn't die of anything catching," said old Joe, stopping his work and looking up.

"Don't you be afraid of that," said the cleaning woman. "As unpleasant as he was, I'd never have hung around him for such things, if he did.

Ah! You can look over that shirt till your eyes hurt, but you won't find a hole in it, nor a worn place. It's the best one he had, and a fine one, too. They were going to bury him in it, but I took it off him and put on a cheap cotton one."

Scrooge listened in horror. He watched what was going on with a hatred and disgust.

Old Joe brought out a bag of money and counted out their payments on the ground.

"Ha, ha!" laughed the cleaning woman. "This is the end of it, you see! He frightened everyone away from him when he was alive, to profit *us* when he was dead! Ha, ha, ha!"

"Spirit!" said Scrooge, shaking from head to foot. "I see, I see. The same thing that happened to this poor man could happen to me. My life seems to be moving in that direction, now... Merciful Heaven, what is this?"

He drew back in terror, for the scene had changed!

CHAPTER TWELVE

The Third Spirit—Mourning

Scrooge was almost touching a bed—a bed without its curtains—on which, beneath a ragged sheet, there lay a something covered up.

The room was very dark, too dark to be seen very clearly, but a pale light from somewhere shone on the bed. And on it, robbed and left alone, was the body of this man—with no one to watch over it, no one to weep for it.

Scrooge looked at the Phantom. Its hand was pointed to the head of the dead body. The sheet was loosely thrown over it, and Scrooge could have easily uncovered the face. Yet he could not make himself do it. He just stood looking at it.

Here was this selfish, greedy, man, thought Scrooge, but what good had all his money done him? He lay in the dark, empty house with not a man, a woman, or a child to mourn or say: "He was kind to me once, and because of that one kind word, I will be kind to him."

A cat was tearing at the door, and there was a sound of gnawing rats under the fireplace.

"Spirit," Scrooge said, "this is a horrible place. Let us leave it! I shall not forget its lesson, believe me. Let us go!"

Still the Ghost pointed its finger at the head.

"I understand you," Scrooge said, "and I would uncover it, if I could. But I don't have the willpower, Spirit. I can't do it."

The Ghost just kept looking at him.

"Are there any people in the town who care anything about this man's death?" asked Scrooge, quite upset. "Show them to me, Spirit. Show me what they are feeling about it, I beg you!"

The Phantom spread its dark robe before him for a moment like a wing. Then he withdrew it and revealed a room by daylight where a mother and her small children were. Scrooge watched carefully.

The woman looked worried. She walked up and down the room, jumped at every sound, looked out of the window, and glanced at the clock. She was even too nervous to enjoy the children in their play.

At last a knock was heard. She hurried to the door, and met her husband. When she asked him faintly whether the news he had was good or bad, he didn't seem to know how to answer.

"Are we ruined? Will we lose all that we have?" she asked anxiously.

"No. There is still hope, Caroline."

"If that awful man gives us a bit more time to pay our debt, there is hope," she said. "But that would be a miracle."

"He is past doing that," said her husband. "He is dead."

She was thankful in her soul to hear it, and said so. Then she was sorry she had said it and prayed for forgiveness, but it had been the true feeling of her heart.

"If he is dead, whom do we owe our debt to now? Who will want our payments?"

"I don't know, Caroline. But by the time that is decided, we shall be ready with the money.

And no future debt collector will be as mean and heartless as *he* was. We may sleep tonight with lighter hearts!"

Yes. Their hearts were lighter. Even the children's faces were brighter. It was a happier house. The only feeling about the death of the man the Ghost had shown Scrooge was one of *happiness!*

"Take me to some other home," Scrooge begged of the Spirit. "Let me see some tenderness and mourning connected with death. Otherwise, the thoughts of that body in that dark bedroom will haunt my mind forever."

The Ghost took him through several streets familiar to Scrooge. As they went along, he looked to see if could find himself anywhere. But nowhere was his future self to be seen. Before long, they came to poor Bob Cratchit's house and went in. The mother and the children were seated around the fire.

The room was very quiet. The mother and her daughters were busy sewing, but more quietly than usual. The noisy little Cratchits sat as still as statues looking up at Peter, who held a Bible. Scrooge heard him reading to them.

" 'And He took a child, and sent Him to be among them,' " read Peter.

The mother laid her work on the table. She was thinking about poor Tiny Tim. She put her hand up to her face to hide her tears.

"It must be near time for your father to come home," she said, when she had stopped crying.

"A little past time," Peter answered, closing his book. "But I think he has walked a little slower than usual these few last evenings, Mother."

They were very quiet again. At last she said, "He used to walk with"—she stopped for a second to get control of herself—"he used to walk, with Tiny Tim on his shoulder, very fast indeed."

"Yes! Yes, he did!" cried the others. "Often."

"But he was very light to carry," she went on, keeping her eyes on her sewing. "His father loved him so that it was no trouble—no trouble. And there is your father at the door!"

She hurried to meet him as he came in. His tea was ready, and they all tried to be the first to serve it to him. Then the two young Cratchits got on his lap, and each child pressed a little cheek against his face, as if to say: *Don't mind it, Father. Try not to be too sad!*

Bob was cheerful with them and spoke pleasantly to all the family. He looked at the sewing on the table and praised the skill and speed of Mrs. Cratchit and the girls.

"The little suit you are making will be done long before Sunday," he said.

"Sunday!" said his wife. "Then, you went today to the cemetery to make arrangements, Robert?"

"Yes, my dear," returned Bob. "I wish you could have gone. It would have done you good to see how green and peaceful a place it is. But you'll see it often. I promised him that we would walk there on Sundays. My little, little child!" cried Bob. "My little child!"

He broke down crying all at once. He couldn't help it. He had loved Tiny Tim too much to hold back the tears any longer.

He left the room and went upstairs into the room above, which was lighted cheerfully and decorated for Christmas. There was a chair set close beside the child, and there were signs of someone having been there lately. Poor Bob sat down in the chair and kissed the little face. He stayed awhile, then went downstairs again, feeling more at peace.

They gathered around the fire and talked. Bob told them how kind Mr. Scrooge's nephew had been when he had met him on the street that day.

"I had only met him once before," said Bob, "and yet, he saw right away that I looked a little sad, and asked what might have happened to upset me. When I told him, he said he was deeply sorry to hear it and offered to help in any way he could. He even gave me his address and invited me to visit him. I have never met anyone so good and sincere. It really seemed as if he had known our Tiny Tim, and felt our sadness with us."

"I'm sure he's a good soul," said Mrs. Cratchit.

"He is, my dear," said Bob. "I wouldn't be at all surprised if he found a good job for Peter."

"Oh! Listen to that, Peter!" said Mrs. Cratchit.

"And then," cried one of the children, "Peter will find a young lady, and start thinking about leaving us and finding a home of his own."

"Oh, stop that!" said Peter, grinning.

"It's quite possible," said Bob, "one of these days, but there's plenty of time for that, my dear. But whenever we do part, I am sure none of us will forget poor Tiny Tim—will we—or this *first* parting that our family has had to go through?"

"Never, Father!" they all cried.

"And I know," said Bob, "I know, my dears, that when we remember how patient and gentle he was—although he was a little, little child—we shall not argue easily among ourselves, and forget poor Tiny Tim in doing it."

"No, never, Father!" they all cried again.

"I am very happy," said Bob. "Very happy!"

Mrs. Cratchit kissed him, the young Cratchits kissed him, and Peter and he shook hands.

Spirit of Tiny Tim, the sweet, simple nature of your soul was surely a gift from God!

CHAPTER THIRTEEN

The Third Spirit—The Tombstone

"Ghost," said Scrooge, "we, too, are soon to part. I know it, but I don't know how. Tell me, who was that man we saw lying dead?"

The Ghost of Christmas Yet To Come carried him, as before (though further into the Future, Scrooge thought) back into the city. Suddenly, Scrooge begged it to stop for a moment.

"This street," said Scrooge, "through which we hurry now, is where I work, and have for a long time. I see the building. Let me see myself. Show me what I shall be in the future."

The Spirit stopped. The hand was pointed in another direction.

"The building is over there," Scrooge said. "Why do you point away?"

The finger did not change.

Scrooge hurried to the office window and looked in. It was an office still, but not his. The furniture was not the same, the man in the chair was not himself.

"Why...? Where have I gone?" asked Scrooge.

The Phantom pointed once again, and Scrooge traveled with it until they reached an iron gate. Scrooge saw that it was a graveyard. That wicked, greedy man that died, the one no one seemed to care about, must be buried here, thought Scrooge. Now I will learn his name.

It was a dark, walled-in miserable place, overrun with weeds, filled more with darkness than light, more with death than life—the right kind of place for such a mean man, whoever he was!

The Spirit stood among the graves, pointing directly at one of them. Trembling, Scrooge moved toward it and stopped.

"Before I go nearer to that gravestone to which you point," said Scrooge, "answer me one question. Are these the shadows of the things that *Must* be, no matter what, or are they shadows of things that *Might* be, only?"

Still the Ghost pointed downward to the grave by which it stood.

"An evil man's actions must lead him to the final end he deserves," said Scrooge. "But, tell me, Spirit, if a man changes his actions, is it possible that the end might also be changed? Is this the lesson you are teaching with these future shadows you show me?"

The Spirit said nothing.

Scrooge crept toward the dark, lonely grave, trembling as he went. And following the Spirit's finger, he saw on the stone a name—his *own* name—EBENEZER SCROOGE.

"Am *I* that man who lay under the sheet on that dark bed?" Scrooge cried.

The finger pointed from the grave to him, and back again.

"No, Spirit! Oh, no, no!"

The finger did not move.

"Spirit!" he cried. "Hear me! I am not the man I was. Because of the lessons I have learned, I have changed. I will be a different person, a better person. Why show me this if I am past all hope?"

For the first time, the silent Spirit's hand seemed to shake.

Scrooge fell to his knees.

"Good Spirit," he cried, "show me pity. Promise me that I still have time to change these Future shadows you have shown me, by changing my Present life."

The kind hand trembled.

"I will honor Christmas in my heart, and try to keep it all the year. I will live in the Past, the Present, and the Future. The Spirits of all Three shall be at work within me. I will not shut out the lessons that they teach. Oh, tell me I may wash away the writing on this stone!"

Holding up his hands in a last prayer that his Future could be changed, he saw the Phantom shrink and disappear. In its place he saw only a bedpost.

CHAPTER FOURTEEN

The End of It

Yes! And it was his own bedpost, his own bed, his own room! Best and happiest of all, his Future was still ahead of him. There was still Time— Time left for him to become a better person!

"I will live in the Past, the Present, and the Future!" Scrooge repeated, as he scrambled out of bed. "The Spirits of all Three shall be at work within me. O Jacob Marley! Heaven and the Christmas Time be praised for this! I say it on my knees, old Jacob, on my knees!"

He was so thrilled with his good feelings and promises that his broken voice would hardly form a word. His face was wet with tears.

"They are *not* torn down!" cried Scrooge, folding one of his bed curtains in his arms. "They are not torn down, rings and all! They are here—I am here—the shadows of the things that *might* have been may be driven away and changed. They will be. I know they will!

"I am so excited I don't know what to do!" cried Scrooge, laughing and crying at the same time. "I am as light as a feather, I am as happy as an angel, I am as merry as a schoolboy. A MERRY CHRISTMAS to everybody! A HAPPY NEW YEAR to all the world! Hallo here! Whoop! Hurray!"

He rushed happily into the living room and stood there—completely out of breath.

"There's the teapot on the warming shelf!" cried Scrooge. "There's the door through which the Ghost of Jacob Marley entered! There's the corner where the Ghost of Christmas Present sat! There's the window I looked out and saw the wandering phantoms! It's all right! It's all true! It all happened! Ha, ha, ha!"

Really, for a man who had not laughed for so many years, it was a wonderful laugh, a most perfect example of a laugh. The first of many laughs yet to come.

"I don't know what day of the month it is!" said Scrooge. "I don't know how long I've been among the Spirits. I don't know anything. I'm just like a newborn baby. Never mind. I don't care. I'd rather be a baby. Hurray! Hurrah! Hallo!"

His happiness was interrupted by the church bells ringing out more joyously than ever he had heard them. Clash, clang, hammer! Ding, dong, bell! Bell, dong, ding! Hammer, clang, clash! Oh, beautiful, glorious sounds!

He ran to the window and put his head out. No fog, no mist—clear, bright, cheerful, crisp, and cold! Golden sunlight! Heavenly sky! Sweet fresh air! Merry bells! Oh, glorious! *Glorious!*

"What's today?" cried Scrooge, calling down to a boy in Sunday clothes.

"WHAT?" replied the boy, as if he couldn't believe such a silly question.

"What's today, fine fellow?" shouted Scrooge.

"Today? Why, it's Christmas Day!"

"It's Christmas Day!" said Scrooge to himself. "I haven't missed it. The Spirits have done it all in one night. They can do anything they like. Of course they can. Of course they can. Hallo, my fine fellow!"

"Hallo!" returned the boy.

"Do you know where the poultry shop is, two streets down, at the corner?" Scrooge asked.

"I certainly do," replied the lad.

"An intelligent boy!" said Scrooge. "A remarkable boy! Do you know whether they've sold the prize turkey that was hanging up there?"

"What, the one as big as me?" said the boy.

"What a delightful boy!" said Scrooge. "It's a pleasure to talk to him. Yes, my lad!"

"It's hanging there now," replied the boy.

"Is it?" said Scrooge. "Go and buy it."

"Right!! You want *me* to go and buy it!" said the boy, laughing. "Well, if it's you that wants it, *you* go buy it!"

"No, no," said Scrooge, "I am serious. Go and buy it, and have their delivery man bring it here, so that I may tell him where to take it. Come back with the man, and I'll give you a big tip. Come back with him in less than five minutes, and I'll double your tip!"

The boy was off like a shot.

"I'll send it to Bob Cratchit's!" giggled Scrooge merrily, rubbing his hands. "He won't know who sends it. It's twice the size of Tiny Tim."

His hand shook as he wrote his clerk's address, but, somehow, he got it written. Then he went downstairs to open the street door and wait for the man from the poultry shop. As he stood there at the door, the knocker caught his eye.

"I shall love it, as long as I live!" cried Scrooge, patting it. "I hardly ever looked at it before. What an honest expression it has in its face! It's a wonderful knocker!—Here's the turkey! Hallo! Whoopee! How are you? Merry Christmas!"

It *was* a turkey! A *heavy* turkey! He never could have stood upon his legs, *that* bird.

"Why, you cannot carry that to Camden Town," said Scrooge. "You must have a cab."

The chuckle with which he said this, and the chuckle with which he paid for the turkey, and the chuckle with which he paid for the cab, and the chuckle with which he tipped the boy, were not nearly as big as the chuckle with which he plopped in his chair and laughed till he cried.

Shaving was not easy, for his hand was still shaking. (And you have to be careful when you're shaving, even when you're *not* laughing and dancing.) But if he had cut the end of his nose off, he would have bandaged it, and been quite happy.

He passed the door a dozen times before he had the courage to go up and knock. But he made a dash, and did it.

"Is your master at home, my dear?" Scrooge said to the girl. Nice girl! Fine girl!

"Yes, sir."

"Where is he, my love?" said Scrooge.

"He's in the dining room, sir, along with Mother. I'll show you in, if you please."

"Thank'ee, just the same. He knows me," said Scrooge, with his hand already on the dining room doorknob. "I'll go in here, my dear."

He turned it gently and slipped in.

"Fred!" Scrooge called to his nephew.

"Bless my soul!" cried Fred. "Who's that?"

"It's I. Your Uncle Scrooge. I have come to dinner. Will you let me in, Fred?"

Let him in?! It is a wonder his nephew didn't shake his arm off! Scrooge felt completely at home in five minutes. Nothing could be more comfortable. Fred's wife looked just the same. So did Topper when *he* came. So did the plump sister when *she* came. So did everyone when *they* came. Wonderful party, wonderful games, wonderful togetherness, *won*-der-ful happiness!

But Scrooge was early at the office the next morning. Oh, he was early there. If he could only be there first and catch Bob Cratchit coming late! That was the thing he most wanted to do.

And he did it! Yes, he did! The clock struck NINE. No Bob. A quarter past. No Bob. He was a full eighteen minutes and a half late. Scrooge sat with his door wide open, so he could see him come into the small office.

Cratchit's hat was off before he opened the door. His long scarf, too. He was on his stool in a jiffy, working away nervously with his pen, as if he were trying to make up for his lateness.

"Hallo!" growled Scrooge, in his old voice, as near as he could fake it. "What do you mean by coming here at this time of day?"

"I am very sorry, sir," said Bob. "I *am* late."

"You are!" repeated Scrooge. "Yes. I think you are. Come here, sir, if you please."

"It's only once a year, sir," pleaded Bob, appearing from his tiny office. "It won't happen again. I was making rather merry yesterday, sir."

"Now, I'll tell you what, my friend," said Scrooge. "I am not going to put up with this sort of thing any longer. And therefore…"

At this, Scrooge leaped from his stool, and gave Bob such a dig in the ribs that he staggered back into his office. "…And therefore, I am about to *raise your pay*!"

Bob trembled. He thought, for a moment, of calling to the people in the street for help. He thought Scrooge had lost his mind.

"Merry Christmas, Bob!" said Scrooge with great kindness, as he slapped him on the back. "A merrier Christmas, Bob, my good fellow, than I have given you for many a year! I'll raise your pay, and try to help your poor family, and we will talk about it this very afternoon, over a bowl of hot punch. Make up the fires good and warm, and buy a coal box for your own office before you do another thing, Bob Cratchit!"

Scrooge kept all his promises and did much, much more. And to Tiny Tim, who did NOT die, he was like a second father. He became as good a friend, as good a master, and as good a man, as the good old city knew, or any other good old city, town, or district, in the good old world.

Some people laughed to see the change in him, but he let them laugh, and paid little attention to them. He knew that some people would not understand anyway. He thought it just as well that they should wrinkle up their eyes in grins instead of frowns. His own heart laughed—and that was plenty enough for him.

As I said to begin with, Marley was dead, to begin with—and he still is, to end with. So, what has changed? Well, what has changed is that neither his Ghost nor the Three Spirits ever had a need to visit Scrooge again. They had shown him the true meaning of Christmas, and he never forgot their message. A new and greater Spirit now lived within his heart. And it was always said of Scrooge that he knew how to celebrate Christmas well—as well as any man alive. May that be truly said of us, and all of us! And so, as Tiny Tim said, *God Bless Us, Every One!*

THE END

CHARLES DICKENS

Charles Dickens was born in 1812 in Landport, Portsea, England. His family was always in debt, and—with their eight children—they had to move from place to place. His father was put into debtor's prison. Young Charles left school and came to know the horrors of poverty, child labor, and the workhouse system.

Through good fortune, the Dickens family came into a bit of money and Charles was able to go back to school. Later, he worked as a clerk for a lawyer, and then as a newspaper writer, reporting on court cases and the workings of the government.

Everything he had experienced, seen and learned went into his own stories, published in magazines as "Sketches by Boz." Dickens was an instant success. He went on to write short stories and novels that became widely famous, including *Oliver Twist* (1838), *A Christmas Carol* (1843), *The Cricket on the Hearth* (1845), *David Copperfield* (1850), *A Tale of Two Cities* (1859), and *Great Expectations* (1861).

Dickens' colorful characters, witty writing style, and surprising plots brought to light the conditions of the poor and helpless and brought about changes to the laws throughout England. He was still working and actively writing up to his death in 1870.